My "e" Sound Box®

WRITTEN BY JANE BELK MONCURE • ILLUSTRATED BY REBECCA THORNBURGH

The Child's World®
childsworld.com

Published by The Child's World®
1980 Lookout Drive • Mankato, MN 56003-1705
800-599-READ • www.childsworld.com

ISBN HARDCOVER: 9781503823082
ISBN PAPERBACK: 9781503831308
LCCN: 2017960300

Printed in the United States of America
PA02371

A NOTE TO PARENTS AND EDUCATORS:

Magic moon machines and five fat frogs are just a few of the fun things you can share with children by reading books with them. Reading aloud helps children in so many ways! It introduces them to new words, motivates them to develop their own reading skills, and expands their attention span and listening abilities. So it's important to find time each day to share a book or two . . . or three!

As you read with young children, you can help develop their understanding of how print works by talking about the parts of the book—the cover, the title, the illustrations, and the words that tell the story. As you read, use your finger to point to each word, modeling a gentle sweep from left to right.

Simple word games help develop important prereading skills, including an understanding of rhyme and alliteration (when words share the same beginning sound, such as "six" and "sand"). Try playing with words from a book you've just shared: "What other words start with the same sound as moon?" "Cat and hat, do those words rhyme?" The possibilities are endless—and so are the rewards!

My "e" Sound Box®

This book concentrates on the short
"e" sound in the story line. Words
beginning with the long "e" sound
are included at the end of the book.

Little  had a box. "I will find things

that begin with my **e** sound," he said.

"I will put them into my sound box."

Little found eggs.

He found lots and lots of eggs.

Did he put the eggs into his box? He did.

Little  found elves.

The elves danced and danced.

Did Little  put the elves into the
box with the eggs? He did.

The elves played with the eggs.

"Be careful, elves," said Little .

Now the box was heavy.

So Little  found an elephant.

"Hop on!" said the elephant.

The elephant went up and down.

The eggs fell out of the box.

The elves fell, too. So did Little e.

"That was a bad bump!" he said.

"What a mess!" said Little

"Now who will help me fill my box?"

An  Eskimo came by.

"I will help you fill your box," said the Eskimo.

"I know where we can find lots
of eggs," said the Eskimo.

Guess who had eggs for Little ?

Guess who had pretty eggs for everyone?

Little 's Word List

egg

elves

elephant

Eskimo

Other Words with the Short  Sound

eggplant

elevator

engine

elbow

elk

envelope

Words with the Long  Sound

Little "e" has another sound in some words. He says his name, "e."
Can you read these words? Listen for Little "e's" name.

eagle

Easter

emu

ear

eel

eraser

More to Do!

Little  asked an elephant to help him carry his box of eggs and elves. Elephants are very big. Elves are very small. Can you answer these puzzles about elves and elephants?

Puzzle: Eddie Elephant is 9 feet (3 m) tall. Ellie Elf is 2 feet (less than 1 m) tall. Which one is taller? How much taller?

Answer: Eddie Elephant is 7 feet (2 m) taller.

Puzzle: Eddie Elephant weighs 8,040 pounds (3,647 kg). Ellie Elf weighs 40 pounds (18 kg). Who weighs less? How much less?

Answer: Ellie Elf weighs 8,000 pounds (3,629 kg) less.

Here are some silly riddles about elves
and elephants!

Riddle: What weighs a ton (907 kg) and wears glass slippers?
Answer: Cinderelephant.

Riddle: What's the first thing elves learn in school?
Answer: The "elf"-abet.

Riddle: How do you know there are three elephants in your
refrigerator?
Answer: The door won't close!

Riddle: How many elves does it take to change a lightbulb?
Answer: Ten! One to change the lightbulb and nine to
stand on each other's shoulders!

Riddle: What do elephants do for fun?
Answer: Watch "ele"-vision.

Riddle: What kind of bread do elves make sandwiches with?
Answer: Shortbread.

About the Author

Best-selling author Jane Belk Moncure (1926–2013) wrote more than 300 books throughout her teaching and writing career. After earning a master's degree in early childhood education from Columbia University, she became one of the pioneers in that field. In 1956, she helped form the Virginia Association for Early Childhood Education, which established the first statewide standards for teachers of young children.

Inspired by her work in the classroom, Mrs. Moncure's books became standards in primary education, and her name was recognized across the country. Her success was reflected not only in her books' popularity with parents, children, and educators, but also by numerous awards, including the 1984 C. S. Lewis Gold Medal Award.

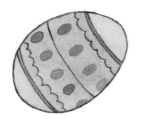

About the Illustrator

Rebecca Thornburgh lives in a pleasantly spooky old house in Philadelphia. If she's not at her drawing table, she's reading—or singing with her band, called Reckless Amateurs. Rebecca has one husband, two daughters, and two silly dogs.